tunnels By Gail Gibbons

Holiday House · New York

For Bill Mitler

Copyright © 1984 by Gail Gibbons
All rights reserved
Printed in the United States of America
First Edition

Library of Congress Cataloging in Publication Data

Gibbons, Gail.
Tunnels.

Summary: A brief introduction to tunnels—their types, shapes, and parts, and how they are built.
1. Tunnels—Juvenile literature. [1. Tunnels]
I. Title.
TA807.G52   1984   624.1'93   83-18589
ISBN 0-8234-0507-9

Most tunnels are long holes dug underground.

**Very small tunnels are dug by ants and worms.
They live in them.**

Moles . . .

chipmunks and prairie dogs dig bigger tunnels.

They dig their tunnels with their front feet.

People dig tunnels, too. Some are small and others are big. A small tunnel can be dug with your hands, a spoon, or a shovel.

Most tunnels are dug by beginning in the middle and digging both ways, or digging from the ends to meet in the middle.

**There are four types of big tunnels made by people.
A rock tunnel is drilled and blasted through solid rock.**

The walls and ceiling stay up because the rock is so hard it supports itself.

A soft ground tunnel is dug through sand, clay, or wet ground.

It needs support so it won't collapse.

Most underwater tunnels are dug through mud.

Their support must be very strong to hold the wet soil and water pressure from above.

A cut-and-cover tunnel is the easiest to build. A deep, wide trench is dug.

After the passageway is built, it is covered up with dirt.

A tunneling machine cuts through dirt and rock.

The dirt and rock are moved away on a conveyor belt.

A new tunnel is being built.

They are hauled away by trucks.

The rock and dirt are lifted up the shaft.

A train carries the rock and dirt to the shaft of the tunnel.

Supports hold the top and sides in place.

It will take a lot of work and time to finish.

Circular Tunnel

Vertical Sidewall Tunnel

Horse Shoe Tunnel

Basket Handle Tunnel

Big tunnels are built in four different shapes.

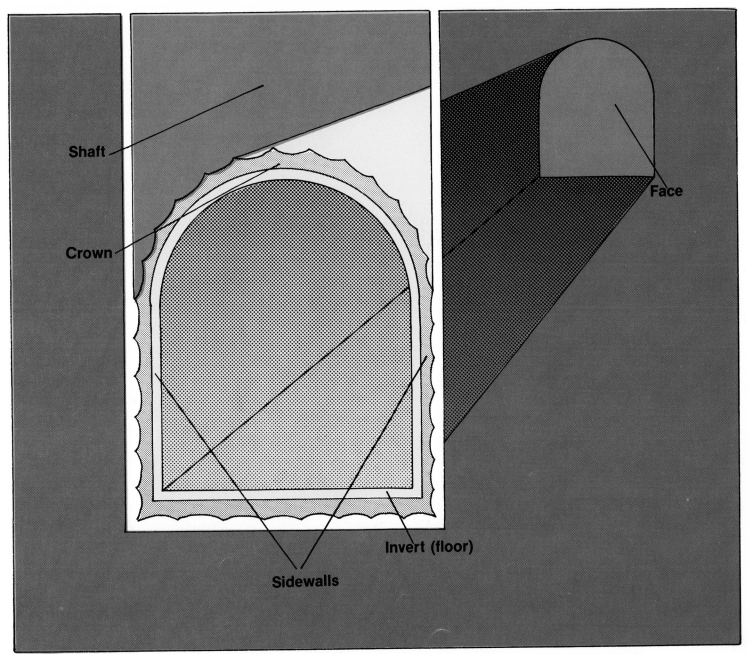

Shaft

Crown

Face

Invert (floor)

Sidewalls

There are names for the different parts of a tunnel.

Tunnels have many uses.
Some tunnels carry water.

Mining tunnels are dug deep in the ground to get coal and metal ores.

Some tunnels go under busy streets.

Others go through mountains.

Subway trains hurry through tunnels under cities.

Tunnels are also built for people to walk through.

Some of the biggest tunnels are built under water.

Animals . . .